Scottish Terrier

Ibizan Hound

Saluki   Chihuahua   Pug   Poodle

Bull Terrier   Chinese Crested   Bulldog   Dalmatian

For El

First published
in 2009 by Macmillan
Children's Books. This edition
published 2018 by Two Hoots
an imprint of Pan Macmillan
20 New Wharf Road,
London N1 9RR
Associated companies
throughout the world
www.panmacmillan.com
ISBN 978-1-5098-4125-7
Text and illustrations copyright
© 2009, 2017 Emily Gravett
Moral rights asserted.

1 3 5 7 9 8 6 4 2

A CIP catalogue record for this
book is available from the British
Library. Printed in China. The
illustrations in this book were created
using pencil and watercolour
www.twohoots books.com

Emily Gravett

Dogs

TW **HOOTS**

I love dogs.

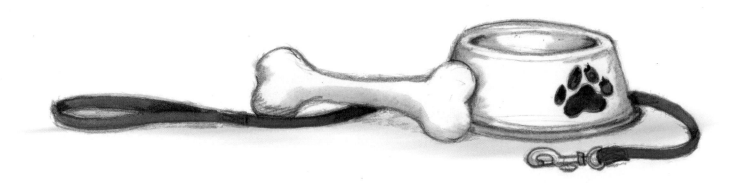

I love big dogs

and small dogs.

I love stroppy dogs

and soppy dogs.

I love dogs that bark

and dogs that don't.

I love dogs that play

and dogs that won't.

I love hairy dogs

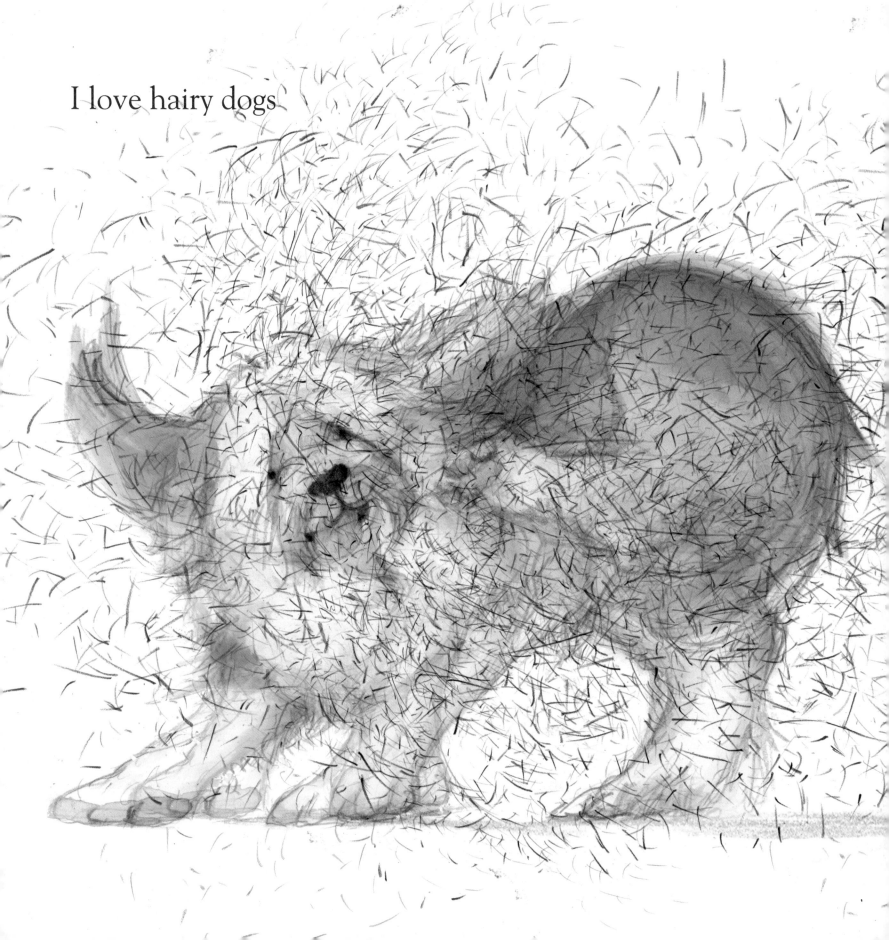

and bald dogs.

Stripy dogs

and spotty dogs.

I love slow dogs

and fast dogs.

Scruffy

and smart dogs.

I love dogs that are good

and dogs that are bad.

But the dog that I love best?
Let's see . . .

. . . is any dog

that won't chase me!

Great Dane

Dachshund

Shar Pei

Bichon Frise   Airedale   German Shepherd   Jack Russell

If you liked DOGS, you'll love . . .

Keeshond

Leonberger